The Fox and the Goat

Retold by Elizabeth Adams

Illustrated by Liliane Oser

W

FRANKLIN WATTS

First published in 2009 by
Franklin Watts
338 Euston Road
London
NW1 3BH

Franklin Watts Australia
Level 17/207 Kent Street
Sydney
NSW 2000

A CIP catalogue record for this book is available
from the British Library.

ISBN 978 0 7496 8529 4 (hbk)
ISBN 978 0 7496 8535 5 (pbk)

Series Editor: Jackie Hamley
Series Advisor: Dr Hilary Minns
Series Designer: Peter Scoulding

Printed in China

Franklin Watts is a division of
Hachette Children's Books,
an Hachette Livre UK company.
www.hachettelivre.co.uk

This kind of story is called a fable. It was written by a Greek author called Aesop over 2,500 years ago. Fables are stories that can teach something. Can you work out what the lesson in this fable might be?

One day, Fox got trapped in a well.

Goat was thirsty and came to the well, too.

"Is it nice in there?"
Goat asked Fox.

"Lovely," said Fox.
"Come in!"

Goat jumped in.

Now she was
trapped, too.

"Stand against the wall and I'll run up your back to get help," said Fox.

Goat stood against the wall and Fox ran up, out of the well.

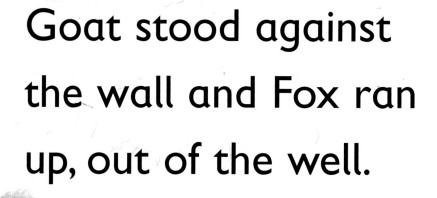

"You said you would get help!" cried Goat.

"Silly Goat!" laughed Fox, and he ran far away.

Puzzle Time!

a

b

c

d

e

f

Put these pictures in the right order and tell the story!

silly sly foolish clever

Which words describe Fox
and which describe Goat?

Turn over for answers!

Notes for adults

TADPOLES are structured to provide support for newly independent readers. The stories may also be used by adults for sharing with young children.

Starting to read alone can be daunting. **TADPOLES** help by providing visual support and repeating words and phrases. These books will both develop confidence and encourage reading and rereading for pleasure.

If you are reading this book with a child, here are a few suggestions:

1. Make reading fun! Choose a time to read when you and the child are relaxed and have time to share the story.
2. Talk about the story before you start reading. Look at the cover and the blurb. What might the story be about? Why might the child like it?
3. Encourage the child to retell the story, using the jumbled picture puzzle as a starting point. Extend vocabulary with the matching words to characters puzzle
4. Discuss the story and see if the child can relate it to their own experience, and perhaps think about the moral of the fable.
5. Give praise! Remember that small mistakes need not always be corrected.

Answers

Here is the correct order!
1. f 2. c 3. d 4. b 5. e 6. a

Words to describe Fox:
clever, sly

Words to describe Goat:
foolish, silly

Now she was
trapped, too.